The Garden Fairy

by Mary S. Gagnon

Acknowledgements

Many thanks to my friends who were such great editors, Carol Denis and Anne Dramko.

Also special thanks to my friend in fairies and fairy consultant, Celeste Crowley.

Table of Contents

5

Chapter 1

The Circle of Stones

"Mom- I don't think you should do that!" There was a little panic in Jackie's voice as her mother pushed the white stones aside and began digging a hole where they'd been.

Mom looked quickly at Jackie, "Why ever not? They're just rocks and I need the space for my roses." The stones began to disappear into the hole she was digging.

"Can I have them?" Jackie asked quickly.

"Sure, honey," Mom's mind was already back into the planting of her first flower garden. Jackie began pawing through the earth for the little white stones. She wasn't sure why her mother hadn't noticed, but the stones had been carefully arranged in an eight-inch circle, and not all the stones were just rocks. Some of them seemed carved, almost like seats and sculptures. Well, no, now that she looked more carefully, not carved, just kind of naturally shaped like seats and sculpture. But still, when she first noticed them they had looked like they'd been carefully placed in a circle.

Jackie's family had just moved into the house this spring. It was a big old Victorian house, with iron gates, and stone borders around the gardens. The house had belonged to just one family since it was built, and the old woman who'd grown up here had died last summer. Jackie's father had seen the for sale sign out front the day it went up. Swish! Their little in-town condo was sold and here they were. Jackie's mother was a frustrated gardener. There had been pots of flowers all over their condo, frequently knocked over by her brothers.

Now her mother was obsessed with digging and planting. While the workmen redid the kitchen and bathrooms, Jackie's mother redid the gardens. The gardens were full of surprises, some surprises were good, like daffodil's sprouting up through dead leaves and crocuses everywhere you looked. Some were not so good, like the woodchuck hole near the back fence or the mouse nest in the water gutter next to the back door. The gardens were full of weeds, the little sculptures and once lovely stone bird baths were either toppled over or chipped and broken. What looked like it had once been a pretty wooden trellis for flowers to climb leaned over awkwardly, held up only by dead vines. Mom called the mess, "possibilities."

Dad had her older brothers, Jonas and Lucas, working in the old carriage house, cleaning it out so they could put the cars in there. They'd claimed it was dangerous, so she wasn't allowed to help. Broken glass, dust and rats, is what she was told. Jackie felt sure that they just wanted to keep any treasures they found to themselves. Her assignment was to help her mother in the garden. That was okay; she liked exploring the yard and the smell of the fresh earth. Maybe there would be treasures out here, too. She'd already discovered those curious little rocks.

Jackie put all the rocks in a little yellow bucket, then took it over to the porch and laid them out. She tried to remember the design they'd been arranged in. With her eyes closed, she could just remember it: a circle of white stones about eight inches across, with a flat area in the center of that. On the outside had been the rocks that looked like chairs and sculpture. When she opened her eyes, the little pile of rocks didn't seem like they would create what she'd seen. She moved them around with her fingers until her mother called for help. Then she scooped them up and put them back in the yellow bucket, leaving them on the porch.

By the end of the afternoon, Jackie and Mom had cleared and planted the side garden with six rose bushes and two sets of seedlings. Mrs. Staples probably would have continued right through dinner if the boys hadn't shown up looking hungry. Some of the gardens would just be cleaned up and left because they had perennials. Others would be replanted. There would even be a garden for some vegetables. Jackie's mother had promised at least one pumpkin patch. Before Jackie went into the house, she glanced back at the new rose garden. For a second she thought she saw movement. A squirrel? A chipmunk? She started towards the garden,

"Jackie!" came Dad's voice. "Time to clean up!" Reluctantly, she went in, leaving the mystery for another day.

It wasn't long before the mystery deepened. First thing in the morning, before they'd even gotten ready for school, Mom had been outside to inspect her rose bushes and seedlings.

"Moles, that's what I think," she was saying to Dad when Jackie came downstairs. "The seedlings are all dug up and two of the rose bushes are knocked over. After all that work!" She sighed, deeply. "Cats! We're getting cats. Today!" Nobody argued with Mom when she was like this. Not that they blamed her. She'd worked hard at the gardens and plus those rose bushes and seedlings cost money.

"Cool!" said Jackie's brother, Jonas. Jonas was two years older than Jackie and in middle school. Both he and Jackie had September birthdays. Except he'd be turning thirteen this fall and she'd be eleven. Jonas had always wanted a cat but they couldn't have one when they lived in the townhouse. "I'm liking this house better and better!"

"What's cool?" asked Jackie's oldest brother, Lucas. Lucas was three years older than Jonas. At sixteen, he was looking forward to learning to drive this summer.

"Moles got into one of Mom's gardens last night, so we're getting cats," reported Jonas.

"Well, that's certainly more environmentally friendly than poisons," responded Lucas. "Do they catch moles?"

"Yes, of course they do," Mom bustled around the kitchen. "We always had cats back home and they caught all kinds of things, mice, rats, bats, squirrels, birds, chipmunks *and* moles."

"Hey," said Lucas brightly, "Maybe I could get a gun, now, and shoot them!"

His father scowled. "I don't think the neighbors would enjoy wondering how good a shot you were. Let's try the cats first. I just hope we don't regret it," was all he added.

When Jackie got home from school she couldn't wait to see the deadly warriors that her mother had gotten at the shelter. She pictured a huge yellow cat with tufts of fur missing from his many battles with local rats. Or maybe Mom would have found a sleek black ninja cat, that would be as still as a statue waiting to strike.

"Where are they?" asked Jackie, dropping her bags as soon as she came through the door.

"Shhh!" said Mom, pointing to a basket. "Aren't they sweet?" The enemies to moles and protectors of rose bushes were asleep in a basket next to the stove. "Mom, those are kittens! I don't think they're going to be killing any moles this summer." Not that Jackie minded. They were adorable!

"They'll grow." Jackie and Mom sat down by the basket, patting the soft sleepy future cats. "Besides, you and your brothers never had kittens. They're a lot of fun. And you'll be surprised, they'll be catching moles before you know it." Jackie couldn't quite picture these balls of fluff as wily hunters, but at the moment, it didn't matter. Besides Jackie had her own idea about what had wrecked the rose garden and it *wasn't* moles.

Chapter 2

The Fairy in the Garden

When Jackie got home from school the first thing she did, after meeting the kittens, was to go look at the damage done to the rose garden. as they called the little side garden where she and her mother had been working the day before. Sadly, the blossoms on the roses that Mom had planted yesterday lay in a pile on the dirt. The Forget-Me-Not seedlings were all dug up, their little hairy roots drying up in the sun. Most curiously, the edge of the garden where the circle of stones had been was now a hole maybe six inches deep and ten inches wide. The rose that had been planted in that spot was no where to be seen.

It was funny her mother hadn't noticed the circle of stones, Jackie thought. She had assumed that her mother had chosen that particular garden to be for the roses, *because of* the cool rock design.

And yet, when Jackie pointed it out to her mother, it was as though she couldn't even see what Jackie was talking about.

"Do you mean that pile of rocks?" is what her mother had said when Jackie pointed them out. How could she not have seen how it was carefully created?

What Jackie had seen was a circle of carefully laid out white patio, a good size for one of her old Barbie dolls. On the outside were short stones alternating with tall stones. On the inside was a surface of neatly fitting flat rocks. It was amazing, old looking and lovely. Then, her mother had dug it up! Just like that! And now this, the garden was wrecked.

"Nope, not moles," said Samantha, Jackie's new friend a few days later. They were looking at the hole in the garden. "They don't dig holes from above ground like this. A skunk would, but I don't smell skunk. Dogs, cats, they all dig.

"Would they come back and dig in the same place?"

"Well, if there was something delicious for them to eat, they would. I don't see anything here that would be tasty to any animal. Why?" Samantha asked.

"Because my mother filled in the hole on Wednesday and again on Thursday afternoon and each morning it was back." The girls stared at the hole.

"The hole was *back?*" Samantha said with surprise. "That's a little creepy."

Suddenly there was a rustle in the weeds and both girls jumped, as first one, then the other kitten leapt out at them, then continued racing across the yard. After recovering from the kittens surprise attack, they got back to the matter at hand.

"Well, I don't know, Jackie." Samantha scootched down by the hole and poked her finger around the edge. "I'm out of ideas."

"I have one." Jackie said, quietly. "I've been seeing a light here after I go to bed. It moves around for a while, then disappears across the field."

"A light? What kind of light, Jackie!" Samantha whispered. Jackie sat down on the ground next to Samantha. She picked at a piece of grass.

"Well, sort of white, and bluish."

"Firefly?" Samantha suggested, knowing the answer before she got it.

"No. Too big and fireflies aren't blue."

"Too early in the summer, too," confirmed Samantha, shaking her brown pigtails. "Say it," she ordered, "Say what you're thinking."

The girls locked eyes. "It's a fairy." Jackie said. Slowly, their gaze returned to the hole. "And she's looking for the rocks."

"Wow," Samantha said, slowly, letting the idea that fairies might be living in her neighborhood soak in. "Fairies."

"Well, one fairy, anyway. And she's not happy that Mom dug up her stone circle." Jackie looked at the poor tattered roses. "What should I do?"

"Well, put the rocks back so she can find them," suggested Samantha.

"I already thought of that. Mom would just throw them out again. When she saw the circle, she thought it was a pile of rocks! I think that they are magic or only kids can see it or something. So we can't put them back here. We should rebuild the stone cirlcle in a hidden spot. Someplace no one would think of looking."

"I like it!" said Samantha. "But where?" Jackie and Samantha got up and scanned the big back yard, then began to wander through it.. Jackie's mother had made progress in some of the gardens, but a lot of them were still full of tall weeds and wild flowers. Bumble bees and honey bees were busy collecting nectar and pollen. Dandelions fought for space with daffodils. The kittens followed the girl's while they toured the yard. Samantha scooped them both up and kissed their heads before setting them down again. They meowed a complaint at having their play interrupted, then bounced through some tall weeds. "Do you think the fairy will be afraid of cats?"

"The old lady who lived here before us had cats, so I don't think so," said Jackie. "I read on-line about fairies and they don't seem afraid of much –except iron. Since people use metal in like *everything,* they don't come near people much anymore. Isn't that interesting?"

Samantha stopped in her tracks. "Jackie, I can't believe we are talking about *fairies*. I've lived here all my life and didn't know there were fairies here. I am *so* glad you moved into *my* neighborhood!"

Jackie beamed. She hadn't wanted to move and leave her old neighborhood. She even had had to switch schools, even though next year they'd all be together again in the 5 – 8 middle school. She had to take the bus to school now when before she had walked. And of course she missed her friends she'd known since kindergarten. But she had to agree with Samantha, this was turning out to be a great neighborhood.

.

"Let's go look for more information about fairies on the internet."

"Look for fairies on the internet!" somehow that struck Samantha funny and she started giggling. Then Jackie started giggling, too.

"What's so funny!" called Jackie's dad. He'd just gotten home from work. He walked over to Jackie and gave her a hug.

"Hi, Mr. Staples," said Samantha.

"Can Samantha stay for dinner?" asked Jackie, "We have some research to do."

"Research? On a Friday? Sounds like you've got a tough teacher!" Mr. Staples exclaimed.

"Oh, um, it's for the garden, you know, the problem with the roses. Can she?" Jackie asked smiling her goofy pretty-please smile.

"Going to be scientific about solving your mother's mole problem, huh? If it's all right with your mother – and Sam's mother, it's fine by me!" Jackie's dad was a "the more the merrier" kind of dad. He always liked having company.

"Thanks, Dad," Jackie gave him a quick hug. She turned to Samantha. "Let's go ask my mother." The girls headed towards the house.

Samantha and Jackie's research hadn't told them much and what it said was confusing. Some said fairies were bad, some said they were good. One place said fairies lived out of the way of humans, or another said they walked through homes if the homes were in the way. No where could Jackie find what she wanted to know. Why didn't her mother see the stones as she had? Why had she just seen them as a pile of rocks, while Jackie had seen them as carefully created patio? Jackie had her suspicions - and a plan.

The sun had just set and Jackie was in her room getting ready for bed. She watched out her window hoping the blue-white light would appear. Kneeling next to her open window with her light turned off, she watched. The little black kitten they were calling, "Java," hopped up on the window sill next to Jackie, purring his heart out. Suddenly, Java was silent. And there it was, out in the rose garden a little light was flickering back and fourth! Java sat stone still as he too watched the light. Jackie was about to open her mouth to call her mother when a second light appeared. The two lights hovered above the ground bobbing slowly up and down.

"*Two* fairies!" Jackie froze. The lights weren't big. If she had to guess, Jackie would have said they were the length of her little finger. They made a soft cotton ball glow. She could have stared at them all night but Java cuffed at the screen and startled her. Remembering her plan, she called, "MMMom! Come quick – I think I see fireflies." Jackie's mother had been down the hall putting clothes away in the boy's rooms.

"Just a minute Jackie," she called back.

"Quick, Mom, before they fly away!"

"I'm coming!" called her mother, bringing the clothes with her. "Where are you looking?"

"Look, Mom – see over there by the roses? I think I see two fireflies – do you see them?" Jackie pointed and Java flicked his short tail. Jackie's mom scootched down next to Jackie and looked over at the rose garden.

"I see the rose garden, but I don't see any lights." She stood up. "Maybe it was just a reflection from the street. Have you brushed your teeth yet?" Mom put the clothes she had in her hands in Jackie's bureau.

Jackie watched out the window as the lights circled each other then rose higher and higher and then disappeared in a streak.

"Huh? Teeth? Yes, I've brushed." She turned away from the window, though Java continued to watch, his black tail swishing back and forth. That answered that.

Chapter 3
An Angry Fairy

"What are you doing here, Effy?" Polt had followed Effy through the woods. He knew all about the destruction of Effy's stone circle. *Everyone* did, she'd complained so much about it! "Effy?"

"Help me dig this up, Polt." Effy was kicking at the new soil that Mrs. Staples had patted over the hole that afternoon.

"Why? You know the stones aren't there." Polt wasn't the type of fairy to get dirty without a good reason.

"I know they're not! But if my stones aren't in this garden, then *nothing* should be!" She grabbed one of the roses and gave it a good pull. A petal came off in her hand.
"If EVERYONE would help me, we could make a wreck of the whole garden! That would teach them! But no! Not one fairy will help." She stopped for a moment mid-air. "Why are you here? Are you going to help me?" she asked, slyly.

"I have no interest in digging up flowers. I like flowers. No, I just wanted to try to get you to forget about this garden. There are too many humans around here now, anyway. Not like when your circle was built." He looked around. "And look at all this iron!"

"This is MY place! Those stones were set up for my mother's mother! I shouldn't have to move! We were here first!" She spun around and the whirlwind she made churned up more dirt.

"Oh, Effy! Someone was here before your mother's mother and someone before her! I know a lovely place where you could make a new terrace."

"THEY TOOK MY STONES!" Effy shrieked as only an angry fairy can shriek.

The shriek blew Polt back a good ten inches. He dusted the dirt from his clean clothes, taking more care than necessary, waiting for Effy to calm down. When she seemed a little sorry, he flew back over to her.

"I'll help you find new stones. It will be fun." Effy knew that she should appreciate what Polt was trying to do. If she had wanted to admit it, he was right. She was just so mad. Mad that the old lady had died. Mad that the old cat had been taken away. Mad that the comfortable garden was being pulled apart. Mad that after two generations of the same family in the house, there was a new family with new children and new cats. Fairies don't like change at all and this was a lot of change!

"I'm still too mad to think about any of that, Polt." Effy finally said. "But, but," she squished the words out, "thank you." She looked at the fresh hole that she had created where her beloved stones had been. "Let's go. I have to think about what I'm going to do next."

Polt smiled brightly, causing his pointed ears to twitch. "Come on, then, I'll race you!" Though Jackie wasn't likely to find it on the internet, the truth is, fairies love competition. They flew up and up and then raced across the field and out of the sight of the house leaving the faintest trail of fairy dust behind them.

The next day was a rainy one, so the Staples stayed inside and made no changes in their new yard. Jackie did go outside briefly to look at the hole that Effy had dug up the night before as well as notice the petals pulled off from the rose bush.

Jackie had no doubt in her mind now that this was the doings of a fairy. The same fairy whose little structure her mother had destroyed. Her mother couldn't see it for the lovely thing it was for the same reason that young people can hear some tones and older folks hear nothing: she was too old. Jackie was certain her brothers wouldn't be able to see the fairies, either. It was all up to Samantha and her.

Even though the fairy was wrecking her mother's garden, Jackie felt sorry for the her. She wondered if setting up the stone circle someplace else really *was* a good idea. Would the fairy find it? Would the fairy just move it back to where it had been? Jackie put the scientific side of her mind to work.

Number one: The fairy might not be content to just dig up a hole every night and might start doing other mischief as time went on.

Number two: Jackie had to do something with the yellow bucket of stones. They were probably magical and who knew what might happen? Also, they didn't belong to her.

Number three: Jackie would have to give the stones back to the fairy and convince the fairy to rebuild somewhere else, or rebuild for her.

Jackie realized she thought of the fairy as a *her*. She hoped it was. She had two brothers and both kittens were boys. It would be nice if the fairy was a she.

She got the yellow bucket from the mud room and rinsed the stones in the upstairs bathroom sink. With a towel from the bathroom under them, she laid them out on her bed and organized them by shape and size. That was easy. There were flat semi-circular stones, triangular stones, square stones and stones the shape of fat crayons, without the points, maybe two inches tall. For a flat surface, she slid a book of fairy tales under the damp towel. They gleamed white. They seemed to Jackie happy not to be dirty anymore. Of course that was silly, Jackie thought, they were rocks, but then again, they belonged to a fairy, which by itself was not exactly sensible.

She played with the stones for some time, trying this way and that to get them to resemble the design she saw before her mother had destroyed it. She couldn't get any design to fit exactly, maybe some of the stones got left behind or maybe it never did fit together perfectly. Or maybe there was some magic involved.

"What are you doing?"

Jackie was so startled by her brother, Jonas's voice that she knocked the stones helter-skelter.

"What are these?" Jonas picked up one of the stones from the floor and turned it over in his hand. Jonas had the same crazy curly hair that Jackie did and it didn't look like he'd had any interest in combing it today. The white kitten that they had named "Lotto" jumped up on the bed and sniffed the stones. He then settled down, paws tucked under and began to purr.

Jackie knew that plain half-truths were usually enough to satisfy her brother's questions. "They are white stones I found in the rose garden," said Jackie simply.

"In the garden where the hole keeps coming back?" Jonas asked, picking up another stone.

"Yup." Jackie hoped that would be the end of his interest. She began putting the stones back in the yellow bucket.

"It's strange that every time Mum fills the hole in, the next day the hole is back," Jonas said as he helped collect the stones. "It's almost like someone is looking for something… maybe these stones."

"Who'd be looking for white rocks, Jonas?" Jackie tried to sound sensible even though she was really nervous. "It's not like they're rare."

"Hmm, these aren't ordinary white rocks, Jackie. Even the cats can see that." Java had settled in next to Lotto and was also purring. It did seem that the stones were having some influence on the kittens.   Jackie's heart began pounding. Did Jonas see what she saw?

"Maybe the question isn't, 'who' would want these rocks, but 'what?'" said Jonas. He ran his hand over the whole pile of stones.

"A raven?" said Jackie quickly. "They like shiny things."

"Yeah, *maybe*," said Jonas, and then suddenly he lost interest in the stones. "So, what did I come in here for? Oh, it's lunchtime."

"Okay, I'll be right down," Jackie called after Jonas as he was leaving her room.

"Whew! That was strange," she whispered to the kittens. She gathered the remaining stones and put them back in the yellow bucket, setting it on the floor before following Jonas down to the kitchen for lunch. The kittens jumped down from the bed and sniffed the yellow bucket. Then they began cuffing the stones and pulling them out of the bucket one at a time, until Java managed to pull the bucket over. Once they had successfully scattered the stones on the floor, they sat on them, like a chicken on her eggs and fell asleep.

Chapter 4

What to do?

"The smart thing to do," Jackie was saying to Samantha on Sunday, "would be to put the stones someplace in the woods. Then the fairy wouldn't have reason to come here anymore." The girls were walking barefoot around the wet backyard. The rain from the day before had left puddles, but the sun made all the wetness warm.

"Yes, but having a fairy in your backyard, even on a part-time basis, is really cool!" Samantha wanted to see more of the fairies, not less.

"I know, I know, but what would be safest for everyone? The fairy *and* us. You saw on the internet what fairies do when they're annoyed. They tie your hair to the bed when you're sleeping or hide your stuff!" Jackie shook her head.

"Jackie," Samantha asked, "Are you scared?" Jackie didn't answer right away.   "Mmmm," she said, finally, "maybe a little."

I would be," said Samantha. "What if she bites?"

"Bites! But her mouth would be so little!" This thought made them both giggle. They looked at their fingers and imagining how big a fairy bite would be.

"Maybe they don't bite, "said Samantha, "But they know magic and everything!"

"My dad says magic is just science we don't know yet."
Jackie thought for a moment. "Do you think that's true? If it is and
if fairies really do have magic, it means maybe someday we'll have
magic, too."

"Only it would be science then," added Samantha.

"Fairy science." Jackie said, her eyes scanning the yard.
"Look, see that tree over there? If we don't put the stones in the
woods, I was thinking that garden over there might be a safe place,
but now I'm not so sure." The girls wandered over to a spot at the
foot of a ledge that dropped away from the rest of the property. On
the other side of the ledge several pine trees grew. It wasn't a part of
the yard that would ever be mowed by her dad, or would it be dug up
and "flowered" by her mum. It was a hidden corner of the yard near
the carriage house. The girls scooted over the ledge and analyzed the
spot.

"I like it here!" chirped Samantha. "I can't see the house, the
trees make it like a little hide-a-way. It's mossy and smells nice.
Maybe I'll move in here!"

Jackie smiled, "You're too big!"

"Are you going to set up the stone circle now?" asked
Samantha, motioning towards the yellow bucket Jackie had brought
with them.

"We can try," Jackie shrugged. "I can't exactly figure out the
pattern. First we have to clear a place." And so the girls began
clearing away pine needles and moss until they had created a place

that was mostly flat. Jackie dumped the stones to one side and began laying them all flat.

"It's like a puzzle," said Samantha.

"But with no picture! Did I tell you that the kittens napped on them? They knocked the bucket over and then laid on them! Cats are so weird."

"They like them. If a fairy has been using the patio for who knows how long, they probably smell like fairies." Both girls lifted stones to their noses.

"Kind of smell sweet," said Jackie.

"Yeah, like melons and flowers – that flower with the little white bells – Lily of the Valley!" added Samantha. "Cats like nice smells." She brushed her long blonde hair back behind her ear. "I think cats see things we don't. My cat is always looking at things that aren't there."

"They can see the fairies," Jackie said, softly. "When I was watching them out the window Friday night, Java was watching, too. And I think Jonas can see them. At least he could see that the stones were special, not just rocks."

Samantha was surprised. "You didn't ask him?"

"No, I didn't want him to tell me I was imagining things. He can be such a know-it-all. There- it sort of looked like that. What do you think?" They'd arranged the stones so that the small flat ones were in the center and all the others around the edge.

Samantha shrugged. "Good, I guess, but I'm not a fairy, what do I know? Do you think she'll find it?"

"I'll watch tonight. If she doesn't find it – I guess I'll have to show her – somehow."

Just then the kittens showed up. They didn't race up like they often did, but walked quietly and sniffed the stone circle. Lotto tapped one stone with his paw. Then they sat down and waited.

Jackie and Samantha looked at each other. "They know," whispered Samantha.

Jackie nodded. "Let's go before anyone else finds us." Reluctantly, the girls left the hidden garden, the kittens trailing behind.

Jackie sat at her window with binoculars, the kittens perched in the open window next to her. The blue light was flitting back and forth over the rose garden. There was only one fairy tonight, so far. With the binoculars, any doubts Jackie might have had were erased. If Jackie hadn't been able to lean the binoculars against the window, she would have been shaking too much to see her. "A real fairy! A real fairy!" She put down the binoculars long enough to dial the phone that she'd put on the floor next to her.

"Hello? Samantha! Samantha!! I can see her!" The binoculars had been Samantha's idea. "I can see her!"

"What's she look like?"

"Blue – blue dress – I think the wings are white, but they're moving too fast to tell. Her hair... her hair...it's hard to tell, maybe yellow. Can you see anything from your house?"

"No, too many trees." Samantha's house was on the same street, and they'd hoped from her attic, she'd be able to see Jackie's back yard.

"Is she going over to the hidden garden?"

"No, she's just in the rose garden. She looks mad! Mum put a big flat stone over the place where she makes the hole, so I bet she's not happy about that! Oh – there she goes! She's gone now. Did you see her head out to the woods?" Jackie asked.

"Nope, nothing from here."

"Jackie – are you ready for bed, yet?" called Mom.

"Gotta go, Samantha, talk tomorrow!" whispered Jackie. "Almost, Mom!" She quickly ran down the hall and put the phone back next to her parent's bed then ducked into the bathroom. When her mother came up the stairs, Jackie came out of the bathroom with her toothbrush in her hand. "Just brushing my teeth," she smiled.

"Just forget about it," said Polt, with a yawn as he lay on the moss outside of the old tree that was the entrance to their home.

"I can't! It's not right!" Effy kicked at the dried leaves on the ground. A startled squirrel scolded her from a tree.

"Right or wrong, that's the way it is. It's not like the circle was fairy-made. Gran said that the boy of the house made it for her. He fell in love with her when he was little and could still see her. When he got big and couldn't see fairies anymore, he built her the stone terrace hoping she'd come back."

"And she did come back, but by then he couldn't see her anymore. Too old," added Effy.

"I know that she charmed it and added to it, but still it wasn't fairy-made. So the other fairies aren't going to help you get it back.

They don't care. Why do you care so much? Even Gran hasn't been there in years," Polt added.

Effy had to think a moment before she responded. Why *did* she care so much? Then the memories came. "When I was little, Gran took me there to teach me to gather and make paint and spice and such. We'd bring our buckets and baskets and we'd fill them with ingredients along the way. When we got there, we'd use up most of what we'd found making the recipes. I was little and got tired easily. She'd put me to bed in flower petals. When I woke up, she'd have finished what she was doing and have something for me to eat." Effy smiled, remembering.

"She was a great gatherer," Polt agreed. "But that was another time, Effy. The woods came right up to the human houses. There were hardly any metal machines, not so many people. And they were a little afraid of us then. Now the woods have been cut back, there's metal everywhere," Polt shuddered. "What did you do at the terrace anyway?"

"Oh, I would sort ingredients I'd gathered from the flowers, like Gran showed me. It's a nice place for dreaming, napping, listening to the wind..." Effy was motionless for once as she described these things. "It would be a good place to teach other little ones about gathering ..."

Polt reached over and placed his hand on her shoulder. "Effy, there are other sweet places that you can do those things. Let it go."

"No!" Effy spiraled up in the air, suddenly angry. "If they wanted it for themselves, well, that would be one thing. But no! They just wrecked it like it was *nothing!* "

"To them it was nothing! They didn't know what it was!" Polt's effort to calm Effy just made her angrier.

"Maybe the stone circle is gone, but I can make them sorry!" She scooped up an acorn and threw it in the direction of the squirrel she'd upset earlier. The squirrel ducked as the acorn went sailing by and climbed to a higher branch where it began scolding her all over again.

Chapter 5

How to Catch a Fairy

School was over at last! Lucas was busy at his job at a sandwich shop and taking drivers ed. classes. When Jonas wasn't mowing lawns, he was goofing around with his friends or at the pond. Jackie was very nearly brother-free. It's not that she didn't like her brothers, she did. Overall, they were good brothers. But she didn't need them around while she and Samantha were planning their fairy-trapping strategies. They could be nosy – especially Jonas.

"So explain this to me," asked Samantha as she helped Jackie drag the equipment to the rose garden.

"Well, since the fairy hasn't found where we put the stones, we'll have to show her. To do *that*, we'll have to catch her. I told Mum that we're catching the mole! She was glad – look at the mess that fairy made of the rose garden!" Three of the rose bushes had been ripped apart. The branches lay torn, hanging at awkward angles. Leaves had been pulled from the other bushes. "Here's my idea. First, we put this little metal border fence around the garden. It's made out of metal and fairies don't like metal. Then we hide this mosquito netting around the back edge. We tie strings to the front of the netting. When she goes into the garden we yank real hard and the net comes down over her. She can't escape around the bottom because the metal fence is there. We grab her and put her in the new location. Voila! Happy fairy, happy mother!"

"The tent?" Samantha asked, eyeing the red L.L. Bean two-man pup tent Jackie and her dad had set up.

"I asked my parents if we could sleep outside tonight, to keep an eye on our mole trap. Is that okay?"

"I've never slept outside before," Samantha said nervously.

"That's okay. We don't have to. As soon as we catch the fairy, we can go inside and watch from my bedroom. We can say we got scared." Jackie had thought of everything.

The girls spent much of the afternoon discussing the "what if's" in the tent. What if she didn't come? What if she came really late and they were asleep? What if the metal fence scared her away completely? But as with all plans, the "what if" they didn't talk about was the one they should have.

It was about 8:30, the sun had set about a half hour ago and the girls were in position. They were laying on either side of the rose garden with ropes in their hands, watching. They'd practiced and practiced pulling the mosquito net down over the garden and could do it clean as a whistle. Mosquitoes wanted to bite, but the girls had lathered themselves up with organic bug spray, so the hungry insects went unfed. Samantha and Jackie were so excited, there was no chance of them falling asleep on the job. However, they were having a hard time staying still.

"You're making too much noise!" whispered Jackie to Samantha as Samantha scratched her nose for the tenth time.

"I'm sorry – this grass is tickling me!" She reached down and rubbed her knee. "I should have worn long pants!"

"Shhhh! It's about the time she usually shows up…" Samantha stopped her scratching and was still as a statue. When she had lain still about as long as she could and was about to scratch her knee again, a blue-white light came zipping into the garden. The girls couldn't have moved at that moment even if a burning tiger had jumped out at them.

The fairy was about three inches tall. Her wings were white and her dress was dark blue with dark blue trim. At first it was hard to see the color of her hair, but the light, which came from her wings, shone on her hair brightly, and it looked yellow-blonde. Her feet were bare. There was no mistaking the look on her face, she was angry. She hovered over the garden for a moment, Jackie thought she'd seen the metal the fence and that was preventing her from coming closer. But then, she lowered herself to the height of one of the rose bushes that hadn't been harmed much yet and began to pull off the leaves. At that moment, Jackie came to her senses,

"Now!" she whispered and the two girls yanked hard on the rope in the hands. Effy looked up just as the mosquito net fell over the little garden. She flew straight up, lifting the net with her.

"Quick!" shouted Jackie and they grabbed the bottom of the net and gathered it into a bundle. Realizing she was caught, Effy tried to escape by frantically flying first one way, then the other. The plan was to take the fairy over to the hidden garden and simply show here where they had set up the circle. With Effy pulling so hard to get away, it was not as easy as they thought it would be.

"Hold tight!" commanded Jackie.

"I am, but she's strong!" answered Samantha.

Slowly the worked their way towards the hidden garden with Effy using all her power to go in the other direction. The problem began when they finally got her over there.

"Look, little fairy, see what we've done?" cooed Samantha. "See, here are your white rocks. See, this is a better spot for your patio…"

Effy didn't understand them, of course, because she didn't speak English. Some fairies learned, but Effy hadn't. And it didn't matter if she had. Effy only wanted to escape.

"She won't look at it!" cried Jackie. "What are we going to do?" This was one thing they hadn't planned on.

"We need to put her in something like a jar, so we can put her next to it and she can see it. – did you bring home your Native American diorama?" Samantha asked.

"Yes, it's upstairs – what a good idea!" answered Jackie. She had used an old aquarium to build a model of a Passamaquoddy village for school. She'd gotten an A on the project and still had it in her bedroom. "I'll bring it out!"

"NO! Don't leave her with me! I don't know if I can hold her alone. Let's take her inside," cried Samantha.

"What will we say if anyone sees us? We can't say we're bringing a mole in the house!"

"Let's hope no one sees us! Com'mon!"

So they walked slowly towards the house. They looped the excess mosquito net over their arms, hiding the fairy. Jackie opened the back door with her elbow and they moved towards the back stairs.

"You girls inside already?" called Jackie's mom.

"Yeah – uh – too buggy!" replied Jackie. "We're just going up stairs. – We don't need anything!" to Samantha she whispered – "Keep moving!"

"Okay then! Good-night girls!"

"Good-night, Mom."

"Good night Mrs. Staples!"

After that they moved as quick as they could to Jackie's room, Jackie shut the door with her foot, not daring to take even one hand from the bundle of net.

With her elbow, Samantha pushed the cover off the aquarium. "Now what?"

There was no way the mosquito net was going to fit in the aquarium.

"I'll have to grab her. You be ready to put the lid back on." Samantha nodded and slowly released her grip so that Jackie could slip her hand into the yards of net. Effy had no room to flutter, so she was still. Jackie's hand found her and slipped around her body.

"What does she feel like?" asked Samantha.

"Like a bird. Let's get this net out of the way." Just as the net was about to slip to the floor, Jackie wrapped her other hand around the fairy. "Okay, on the count of three, I'll let her go and you close the lid. It's metal, she probably won't want to get too close to it anyway. One, two… Three." And on three Jackie dropped Effy into the Passamaquoddy diorama, complete with wigwams and cooking pots, and Samantha pushed the cover in place, scraping Jackie's fingers in the process.

When they were done, they plopped onto the floor and stared. Effy stared back. All that fighting had tired her out. She sat where she had fallen, breathing hard. She looked from Jackie to Samantha and back again. She'd never been this close to humans before. After a moment, she remembered that she was mad and she disappeared into one of the wigwams, a blue fairy light shining out from the smoke hole.

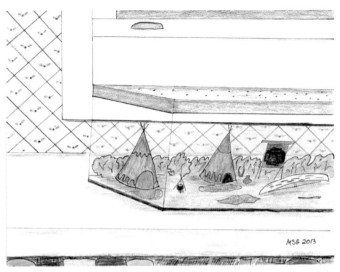

Jackie and Samantha hugged each other. Effy sulked. The thing about fairies is they live a long time. Not forever, but maybe two or three people lifetimes. So it is not important for a fairy to grow up too soon. Of course a fairy's body grows up just as it supposed to, just like all things that grow. However, the way a fairy looks at things, whether it is as a baby, a child, or a middling, this depends on the fairy. People are like this, too. Some understand the world at a very young age. They use grown up words and grown up thoughts before adults would expect them to. On the other hand, there are those people who don't seem to be ready to look at the world in a grown up fashion even after everyone else their age does. Effy was a bit like the second group. The other fairies knew this. She wasn't all that easy to be around. She got mad easily and blamed others for her mistakes and didn't understand other people's point of view. The fairy community was more peaceful when she was out and about.

So it was a surprise when, for the first time in her fairy life, Effy wasn't blaming anyone else for her predicament. She wasn't afraid. These girls meant her no harm, she was sure of that. Soon some fairy would realize that she was missing and some fairy, probably Polt, would come rescue her.

She knew that the only one to blame for being trapped in this glass cage was herself. Being mad at yourself can be much worse than being mad at someone else. So she sat in the wigwam, feeling stupid and foolish and shedding a few tears for good measure.

While Effy was hidden in the wigwam, Jackie and Samantha were doing all they could not to sing and dance. Catching a fairy is not something that happens every day.

"Too bad we couldn't keep her," said Samantha, "like a hamster."

"Some hamster! We don't even know what she eats! She's very strong! I think the only reason she didn't fly out is because the cover is made from metal. Did you see what she looked like? Her ears were pointed!"

"And her hairline started way back on her head. Her wings were almost invisible they were so thin. What did it feel like to hold her?" asked Samantha, a little enviously.

"Well, once I held a baby bird. My friend's pet finch had babies and she was moving some of them to a second cage. I helped catch them. I caught one in my hand and I could feel its heart beating and it was warm and soft. Then it bit me. She sort of felt like that, but she didn't bite." Jackie looked back at the aquarium. "Now what?"

"Yeah, now what?" answered Samantha. "She wouldn't look at the stone circle and now it's so dark I'm not sure she'd even see it if we took her out there. Can fairies see in the dark, you know, like cats?" As though they'd been waiting to hear the words "cats" Java and Lotto pushed the door open and came in. They hopped up on the table where the aquarium was and sat, staring at the glowing wigwam. Lotto turned to Java and sniffed his ear, as though to pass a private message. "The kittens seem kind of, I dunno, respectful of the fairy. They don't act like they would if it *were* a hamster, you know, all excited." Lotto and Java wrapped their little tails around their front paws, sitting patiently and watching.

"I didn't read anything about cats and fairies. At least they don't seem to be enemies. That's good! How are we going to make her *look* at the circle as well as be able to see it in the dark? And this aquarium is too heavy for us to carry." The girl's excitement faded away as they pondered this list of stumbling blocks. The kitten's ears pricked up.

"What's that?" But Samantha didn't need to say anything, they could both all hear it. "She's crying!"

"Then we better figure something out." The girls jumped at the sound of Jonas's voice.

"Jonas," cried Jackie, "What do you want?" She stood up and tried to hide the aquarium behind her.

"To get that fairy to stop wrecking Mom's garden," he said with a smile.

"You know?" Jackie gasped.

"Yup and I know that you rebuilt her little play house over by the pine tree and are hoping she'll leave Mom's garden alone once she sees it set up in a new location. You're also worried that she won't take time to look at it if you just take her over there and let her go. And that maybe it's too dark for her to see it, anyway. So what you need are these glow sticks." Jonas held out a black plastic bag that had a picture of glow sticks on it. "If we put these around the play house…"

"Stone patio!" Jackie corrected.

"Whatever, she'll at least see it. And I can carry the Indian village out to the tree."

Jackie stared at him a moment. "Jonas, how come you can see her? Mom can't."

"Neither can Lucas. I don't know, maybe I'm just not grown up enough yet," he said with a sigh. "But you should be grateful, because you need my help tonight." With that he broke open the glow stick bag and snapped the sticks so that they began to glow. "Hold these," he said to Samantha. As he picked up the aquarium, Jackie said, "Shouldn't we cover it her up? What if anyone sees?"

"Naw, it'll be too suspicious, besides, no one can see her but us. This just looks like you want to play with your Indian village by glow stick light." That worked for the girls, so they followed Jonas down the back stairs, Jonas being careful not to jiggle the fairy too much. Samantha ran ahead and put the glow sticks around the patio. They gave a wonderful magical glow to the white stones.

Effy could feel the glass box being picked up and carried. She stopped crying and peeked out of the wigwam to see where they were going. If they were going outside, maybe she'd get a chance to escape! The three children were talking in soft voices. Even when the bigger boy had showed up, they still spoke softly. Except for their size, they didn't seem fearsome. There were plenty of old stories that were shared around the fires at night about humans who captured fairies and made them do their wishes! Since Effy always thought of herself as brave and strong and clever, she never had worried about coming to any harm at the hands of humans. It was a bit different now that she found herself a prisoner!

Suddenly, their journey ended with a "thump!" Again she peered out of the wigwam. Yes, they were outside. She could see the huge faces watching her. What where they thinking? It was light enough to see that they were in the yard that she knew so well. She ventured out of the wigwam to look out of the glass box. The faces seemed to be looking at something beyond her. She turned around. There, lit up by glowing sticks, were her terrace. Someone, probably those girls, had tried to put it back together – except that this was a new place. She immediately knew where they were. Not in the rose garden where it had been for so long, but further away from the house. Later, when she was safe at home, she would decide that the new spot was a pretty good spot, even if a human had picked it out.

One of the girls was taking the nasty metal top off the glass box and all three children were leaving. They were letting her go! Effy didn't need any time to think this over. Like a flash she was flying top speed back to the oak that marked the entrance to her home.

Jonas, Samantha and Jackie watched the blue light fade across the field. Finally, Samantha said it best, "I'm happy and sad." Jackie nodded. None of them knew what to do next, and they didn't want to talk about it. It was Jonas who broke the spell.   "Come on, I'll make you some popcorn."

Chapter 6

The Fairy Spice

Effy had been slow to tell the others what had happened to her. She didn't want to hear anyone tell her that she had been careless. She knew that herself. She also knew she had been lucky. She also-also knew that they'd make her promise not to go back, and she wasn't sure she could make that promise. For the time being, she busied herself with showing the middlings how to gather materials for paints. Her village was beautifully painted, but needed a lot of upkeep. Sometimes, if they were in the mood, the fairies would also paint things out in the world, just to brighten a dark corner or maybe decorate for a party. Effy was a great gatherer of materials. Because she wandered so much, she knew secret places to find the best ingredients.

Fairies are very clever, this is well-known. Like people, of course, they know the resources of where they live. Effy's fairy folk lived in the Northeast, in the rather *north* of the northeast at that, where winter meant snow and spring meant mud. Being a gatherer, Effy especially loved the seasons. All times of the year were good for gathering. Even the darkest of winter months offered an abundance of good things most would walk by and not even notice. For example most would not see the tiny shoots some trees and bushes were already putting out – very useful in the fairy village. Effy was happy that she had responsibilities that kept her roaming the forest in the winter months, however some fairies had jobs that kept them under the oak tree all winter. For example, Polt was a carver and spent his winters busy inside.

During the summer and autumn, certain fairies hunted for the gems native to the area. They would bring home purple amethyst, green and red tourmaline, blood red garnet and quartz – so much quartz! – in all colors.   In the cold months carvers, such as Polt, would turn the stones into beautiful objects, cups and dishes, furniture, and items to be worn or traded. If they wanted to decorate with gold, they traveled about a day's journey west. A village of fairies there found gold in the Swift River that they lived next to. Not a lot of gold, but enough for their needs. The fairies with gold were usually happy trade for gems from Effy's village.

Now it was late summer, which was the busiest time for gathering. Effy was glad to have the help of the middlings, though sometimes they forgot what they were doing and wandered off following a sweet smell or napping on a warm rock. She'd been teaching them how to follow the honey bees to find blossoming plants all morning. From these plants they took just tiny snips of the inside flower and placed it in their buckets. Effy realized she hadn't heard the chatter of the middlings for a while. She looked around the bush. At first she didn't see them, but straining her ears, she heard snoring. There they were curled up and sleeping on a sunny patch of moss.

The honey bees had lead Effy and the middlings to the edge of the field next to Jackie's house. Effy knew this, but didn't let herself think about it. She had the responsibility of the middlings. However, they were asleep and what would it hurt to just peek at the house? Effy flew up high so that she could have a quick look at the house. No one was about. She thought about the girls who had gone to the trouble to set up the terrace in a new spot for her. And to keep Effy from tearing up the rose garden, of course. She wondered, again, why the girl hadn't kept her in the glass box until she died. That would have saved the garden. Why hadn't the children done that?

"Effy? Effy?" called one of the youngsters, "where are you?" Effy abandoned her wonderings and flew back down to the little fairies.

"I have one more place I want to go, then we'll head back, okay?" Full of energy from their nap, the middlings liked the idea of soon being done with the day's work. They didn't spend much time at the little bog Effy took them to. Effy was too distracted to organize them well and they quickly lost interest. After about as long as it takes to slow-cook a mushroom, Effy told them they'd done a good job and that they'd go out gathering again tomorrow, then sent them home. She headed for a cozy spot she knew. Once, some humans out for a picnic had left behind a glass tea cup. It was filled with leaves and pine needles and Effy had added some milkweed fluff. It was a lovely place for a nap and that's what she needed. She curled up and quickly fell asleep. When she woke up, it was dark.

She knew where she wanted to go and only hesitated a moment. Should she tell someone where she was going? No need, she wouldn't be gone long. Off she went through the woods until she came to the field near Jackie's house. Effy paused here to dim her light. She didn't want to be seen by any human children. The cats, well, they could see her with or without her light, so there wasn't much she could do about that. Cautiously, she approached the house, flying over the lawn, briefly looking at the terrace, then over to Jackie's window. It was the same window that the Indian Village sat in front of. Now that she was here, Effy just wanted to see Jackie. Maybe seeing Jackie would help her understand how the girl thought.

Jackie was already in bed and asleep. Effy stared at the sleeping girl. She didn't look so different from the middlings when they slept, just lots bigger and with funny ears. Watching Jackie sleep didn't tell Effy why the human child had gone to so much trouble for Effy especially when she'd been so destructive in their rose garden. Did any fairy know why humans did what they did?

Effy shook her head and was about to head home when she became aware of something. Effy's fairy eyes could see that there was a pale yellow glow around Jackie. Pale yellow meant that the girl was sick. Pale yellow meant the girl wasn't very sick, maybe a summer cold. Pink or blue would radiate if she were healthy. Fairies get sick, too, but not often because they have good medicine. Effy had been sick once, so she knew the way you felt when you didn't feel good. First one, then the other kitten had found Effy at the window and were sitting respectfully as they always did when they saw Effy.

"Go lay on the bed!" Effy ordered the cats, pointing to Jackie. "Go keep her warm!" The kittens looked from Effy to Jackie then back to Effy, then at one another. They leaped down from the window sill and hopped over to Jackie, nestling themselves next to her feet. Jackie wiggled her feet under the warm cats. Satisfied, Effy flew to the terrace. She settled herself in the center and looked around. The smell of honey and roses met her nose immediately. Someone, no doubt the girls, had left drops of honey on roses petals on one side of the circle. How did they know that was a favorite fairy food? Humans always amazed her. Obviously, they were trying to tempt her to come back. The circle itself was in need of a lot of attention. Jackie hadn't really known how to set it up. Effy couldn't resist putting some of the stones back in their proper places. When she finished, the stones fit together more tightly and it looked much neater. She helped herself to a roseleaf. Not exactly fairy food, but not bad for a snack. After a last look at what she'd accomplished, she flew back to the woods.

A week passed before Effy returned to Jackie's yard. She'd been very busy with the middlings and she had accompanied Polt on some business of his across the woods in the other direction.

It was a lovely summer evening and Effy hadn't planned on ending up at Jackie's. She'd stopped by the brook to say hello to the water sprite. Then she skimmed along the big bog to see how the ducklings were doing and if there were going to be a lot of cat-nine-tails this year. The smell of the small pink apples that hung on the apple trees was heavenly. She found a honey bee that had still been out when the sun set and guided her back to her hive. A fox was getting ready to pounce on an unsuspecting mouse and Effy couldn't resist pulling his tail-fur and making the fox yip. The mouse squeaked when it realized what had nearly happened and disappeared into the tall grasses. Before she knew it, she was in the field behind Jackie's house. Effy slowly circled the field, enjoying the smell of the blossoming Black-Eyed Susans. Without much thought, she headed towards Jackie's darkened window. She landed on the window sill and looked into the room. Jackie was in bed, but not quite asleep. A moment later Jackie's mother was at the door.

"Here, Jackie, take these, they'll help you to sleep." Jackie's mother had two white pills which Jackie took with water.

"Thanks, Mom. I hate being sick in the summer. It's just not fair!"

"I know, honey. I'm sure you'll be feeling better tomorrow. Now get some sleep." Jackie kissed her mother and lay back down. To Effy's eyes, the yellow around Jackie was brighter. Of course Effy didn't know what they were saying, but it wasn't hard to guess. She hoped those pills had strong medicine in them, because she was sure that Jackie was going to need it.

After that, Effy came back almost every evening about the same time. Each night she would watch Jackie, with either Jackie's mother or father helping her to get comfortable. Effy didn't think the pills were much help; it was easy to see that Jackie was getting sicker, not better. There were new pills in different colors. These were pills that a doctor had prescribed, but Effy didn't know that. All she knew was that Jackie's light was getting more and more yellow.

One evening, Polt had come with her.

"I don't think they know what they are doing. She's not getting better," Effy said impatiently.

"Her family looks worried," commented Polt. Even a fairy could see the worry in the human faces. Mom and Dad stood beside Jackie's bed and her brothers peeked through the door. Java and Lotto saw Effy and jumped onto the window sill to be near her. At first Polt was nervous, not all cats get along with fairies. He quickly saw that these kittens were very wise and he knew he didn't need to be afraid.

"What are those cats looking at?" Lucas asked Jonas. "Look, it's like they're looking at something right on the other side of the screen."

Jonas turned his gaze away from his sister to the cats. He stared for a moment, then said, "Ah, who knows. Bugs? Fairies? Birds?"

"Fairies, yeah, Jackie would like that!" Lucas laughed. But Jonas didn't laugh. He looked right at Effy.

"Call the doctor," Jackie's mother was saying to her father. "If he thinks it's a good idea, I think we should take her to the hospital. Lucas, get the car out of the garage," directed Mom, "Just in case."

The humans began rushing around and Effy and Polt could see why. The color around Jackie had changed again. It was a terrible yellow-green.

"That middling is very sick," said Polt. "They better have good medicine or I don't think she'll survive." Now fairies don't much care about what happens to humans. Mostly humans are a bother and in the way. However, even fairies have a soft spot for children. After all, it is usually human children who believe in them and try to do nice things for them.

"If their medicine was any good, she'd be better already," said Effy. "We have to do something."

"Effy! You're not thinking…"

"Yes, I am!"

"But you know what will happen, don't you? I don't think it's a good idea…"

"I am not going to let her *die!* I have to try to help!" Effy turned to the kittens, "Make a hole in that screen!" she ordered. Then she and Polt flew over to the stone circle.

The kittens immediately started digging at the screen with their claws. Although the screen wasn't very strong, fairies do not touch metal, it burns them. If the kittens couldn't make a hole in the screen, Effy wouldn't be able to get in. Effy stood looking at the rose leaves with honey on them that Jackie had left out for her. Because the circle was a special place, the rose leaves had hardly wilted. Effy reached into her bag and pulled out a handful of fairy spice and flung it on the honey. "You, too," she said, sharply to Polt, who pulled fairy spice out of his own pocket and began dropping it on the honey.

"That's it, let's hope that the cats made a hole big enough!" Effy gathered up four of the petals and flew back to Jackie's window. When she got there, there was no hole at all, instead, the screen was up. Effy didn't have time to think about how the cats had managed that. No one was in the room at the moment except Jackie. Effy could hear the other humans calling to each other. Effy flew right over to Jackie's bed. She was about to drop the petals one at a time into her open mouth when Polt grabbed her hand.

"Think about what you are doing, Effy. Be sure you want to do this," he said, staring deep into her eyes.

Although they knew the humans were very near, Effy took the time to take a deep breath. She smiled at Polt, "I'm sure." Then she dropped the honey and fairy spice into Jackie's mouth. Jackie wasn't awake, but she wasn't exactly asleep, either and she swallowed the honey. The adult humans were hurrying into the bedroom. With no time to go back, Polt and Effy flew up to the shelf over Jackie's bed and hid behind the books. Mom wrapped Jackie up in her blankets and Dad carried her out to the car. When everyone had left the room, the two fairies headed for the window. In the reflection on the glass, Effy saw a face. She turned around just in time to catch a glimpse of Jonas, who'd been watching the fairies the whole time. So that's who opened the window, thought Effy. She spun around, making a glowing tail of blue fairy dust, then followed Polt out the window and home.

Chapter 7

The Spring

"You have to eat, Jackie!" Mom pleaded. "You can't live on honey and spring water, sweetheart!" Everyone was so pleased that Jackie was well again, that they didn't mind her strange food cravings at first. The doctors told her mother and father that once she was home, her appetite would return and not to worry. But Jackie had been home a week and still she would eat only honey, spring water and strangely, rose petals. The kitchen was full of food her mother had cooked in hopes of getting her to eat: cookies, cake, fruit, spaghetti, seafood – all her favorites. And Jackie tried to eat, she didn't want her family to be worried anymore. But every bit of food she put into her mouth tasted exactly like paper. After a mouthful, it would stick in her throat and she would spit it out. Although she wasn't hungry, she knew she was getting thinner. Jonas was the only one that didn't try to get her to eat things she didn't want to eat. He just kept buying more jars of honey.

The reason for this honey fixation of course was because Effy had fed Jackie the fairy spice. It had cured her in hours, but left her not able to eat human food. Effy and Polt had known that this would happen. Effy had planned to come right back as soon as Jackie was home and undo what she had done. However, fairy time is different from human time and quite simply, she forgot. She didn't remember until she reached for some fairy spice to sprinkle on a particularly delicious looking nut and saw that the bag was empty.

"POLT!" shouted Effy. She paced anxiously, leaves crunching under her tiny feet. When Polt didn't appear, she closed her eyes and thought his name as hard as she could. Moments later, he swooped down, landing next to her.

"Not so loud, Effy! You gave me a headache! What's the emergency?" Polt rubbed his sore head. Effy ignored his complaint.

"Polt – oh, Polt! I forgot about the human middling – we have to do something – she's probably starving!" Effy wailed.

"Oh, the human girl. Are you so sure the fairy spice made her well? Maybe it was too late and she died," he said, lazily. While Polt cared a lot about Effy, he didn't care much about people.

"Of course it made her well! Why wouldn't it? Now we have to bring her here, to the spring." Effy paced around in circles.

.   Polt stopped rubbing his head and stared at Effy. "We can't bring her here. You know that. Why would you even think such a thing?"

"Well, we certainly can't take enough of the water to her – she's too big! She'll have to drink it directly from the spring. It's the only way." Why couldn't Polt see the sense of it?

"Effy, you can't bring a human here, not even a child. It's not right. Think about it! It's too dangerous for the village! You never think anything through! Never!" Polt, always so patient with Effy, was so angry sparks were coming off his head.

"But you helped me feed her – you knew what that meant…" she pleaded.

"I thought you had another idea, something that wouldn't bring a human near our home." Polt shook his head. "I won't help you, Effy. I just can't." Polt crossed his arms and turned his back to her.

Effy was shocked. Polt had never been angry with her and she didn't like having him angry at her. How easy it would be to forget about the girl and make Polt happy! What good had humans ever done for fairy-folk, anyway? She almost changed her mind, then she remembered Jackie's kindness. If Polt wouldn't help her, she'd go alone. "I'm sorry, Polt, but I have to do this," Effy said, sadly, and flew off into the woods.

Effy hurried to Jackie's window. The screen still had the claws marks on it from where the kittens had tried to dig a hole. She peered into the bedroom and saw Jackie sleeping in her bed, with empty honey jars sitting on the floor. Effy sighed. She hadn't thought through any of the details of her plan.

Plan? What plan? Effy sat down on the window sill with a plop and a sigh. Polt was right, she never thought anything through. How did she think she was going to get the girl from the house deep into the woods? Would she really be endangering the other fairies? But until the effects of the fairy spice were undone, Jackie wasn't truly well, and Effy had to finish what she'd started. All this thinking exhausted the fairy and Effy fell asleep where she sat. She woke up swatting at her nose. There was Polt, tickling it with a feather.

"Polt, oh, you came!" Effy was so happy to see Polt. She jumped to her feet and hugged him. "You're right – I don't think things through! Here I wanted to help this girl, but I haven't any idea where to begin. Please don't be angry any more."

Polt smiled and shook his head. "What do I have to be angry about? I was thinking, "if only you were this way, not that way." Then I realized that you are you, Effy. Nothing I say will change you and I wouldn't want to change you even if I could." Effy blushed at Polt's sweet words. "Plus I didn't think you could do this without me." He looked into the dark room. "So you haven't figured out how to get her out of the house yet."

Effy shook her head. "No. I have no plan at all."

"Well, she's dreaming – see how she's moving? Send her a thought – you're good at that. Put the idea in her head that she should come outside. The house is dark, everyone else must be asleep. This is a good time."

Effy spun around and stared at the sleeping girl. The way she was moving it was easy to see that she was dreaming. "It's a lovely night – come out side and come for a walk!" Effy thought this thought and sent it with all her might. At first nothing happened. Then, slowly, Jackie began to stir. She sat up, stretched and put on her blue slippers.

"Com'mon, Polt, she'll be coming out the door." The two fairies flew to the backdoor and waited for Jackie.

"Is she awake?" asked Polt.

"No, not really. She's dreaming. If she stays asleep, she won't remember the way to the spring."

"Let's do our best to keep her asleep then," Said Polt, relieved. Jackie met them at the backdoor.

"Follow us." Effy said, then to Polt she said, "In a dream, it doesn't matter what language you speak. You're always understood." She turned back to Jackie, "Follow us."

And so they began the trip to the deep woods. Even though Jackie walked quickly, it was much slower than the fairies had ever travelled the distance before. At times they would sit on a branch and wait for her to catch up to them. The fairies were getting tired and hungry themselves, and picked up acorns to nibble along the way. It was the quietest time of the night when they finally reached the spring. Surrounded by white stones and moss, the spring was about six feet across. The moon was reflecting in it and Polt and Effy just stared at it for a moment, soaking in the beauty. Effy sighed and thought to Jackie,

"You must drink this water. Drink until you can't drink another drop."

"I don't have a cup," thought Jackie back.

"Why doesn't she drink?" asked Polt.

"She said she doesn't have a cup," she answered Polt. Then to Jackie she said, "Just sip the water from the spring."

Obediently, Jackie got down on her knees and bent over the water and began scooping it up in her hands. She drank and drank and drank. The fairies were beginning to think she would never stop until the spring was empty, but at last Jackie was full. She burped. Polt and Effy looked at each other in delight.

"Now go home," Effy said, gently to Jackie.

"You think she is just going to go home? We have to lead her!" Exhausted and hungry, Polt's voice showed how tired he was. .

"She can follow the way we brought her. She should remember." Effy was anxious to be done with this human middling, now that she was cured.

It was Polt's turn to kick leaves in anger. "What if she doesn't? Then she'll get lost and people will come here, looking for her!"

Effy was about to say something, but then, Jackie spoke aloud.

"Where am I? What am I doing here? Mom?" Fully awake, Jackie was immediately aware of three things: She was in the forest, she was alone, and she was scared. "Dad?"

Effy and Polt's argument was instantly forgotten. "She's awake!" said Effy with alarm. Neither Effy nor Polt had communicated directly with a human before. While it wasn't forbidden, it certainly wasn't encouraged among the fairy-folk. The urge to hide and let Jackie find her own way home was strong in both of them. Jackie's first awake steps caused her to trip over a branch, and fairies, being creatures with hearts, couldn't bear to see the young girl hurt and afraid. They danced in front of her saying soothing things. Jackie of course couldn't understand what they were saying, but she could see and hear them. Normally, anyone meeting fairies in the forest would be overwhelmed with delight and awe. It is a rare experience to be savored and cherished. Jackie, however, was not in any kind of mood to be impressed by fairies. No longer protected by the fairy magic, the mosquitoes had found her. While her sensible brain told her there were no dangerous animals in her home town, on finding herself in the forest in the middle of the night on a full moon, her less-than-sensible brain was fully in charge. Weasels and bears and moose would surely descend on her at any moment. She took one look at the dancing blue lights and cried,

"Take me home!"

Startled by Effy's words, both fairies darted behind a tree. And while the fairies didn't speak a word of human, her meaning was clear. There was no further discussion between Effy and Polt about what to do next. They brightened their glow and began the way back to Jackie's house, while Jackie followed close behind. During the hike into the forest, the enchantment had prevented her from stumbling. On the way back, fully awake and cleansed of any kind of enchantment, Jackie tripped, stepped on branches, and got eaten by mosquitoes. Fortunately she was scared enough not to think too much about her aches and pains and kept following the blue lights. In human time, probably an hour had passed before they came to the field. When Jackie saw her house, she began to run and the fairies knew that they had accomplished what they had set out to do.

As the houses grew larger, Jackie could see the form of a person standing near the gardens. She slowed down - what if it weren't a family member?

"Jackie!" called out the familiar voice of Jonas. "Jackie?"

"Jonas! I am so glad to see you – you won't believe…" Jackie was running now.

"Yes, I would and it's all my fault!" said Jonas releasing the guilt he'd been holding in.

"Your fault?" she reached Jonas's side. "How was this your fault

"I opened your window the night we took you to the hospital. I knew the fairies wanted to come in and I let them. I thought… I thought they could help you."

"They must have," Jackie responded. "I mean, the doctor's couldn't explain why I got well so fast…so…"

"Yes, but then all you wanted to eat was honey and I figured that was because of them…"

"Honey? I don't remember that." Jackie shook her head. "I don't even like honey so much."

"Well, it's all you've lived on for the past two weeks. It's all you would eat."

"Weird. Well, right now I could eat anything! My stomach is growling!"

"Let me make you a sandwich and you should wash up before Mom and Dad see you. They'll have too many questions if they see you like that!" Jonas pointed at her clothes.

Jackie looked down at herself. Her nightgown was dirty and torn from all her falls in the woods. Her beloved blue slippers were ruined. "I see what you mean."

"You go change and I'll make you a sandwich," directed Jonas.

"Two sandwiches," Jackie insisted.

"Okay, two sandwiches. Then we'll wake Mom and Dad." Jonas laughed with relief.

Jackie turned back to the field. "I can see them, they're watching me. See them?" Jackie pointed towards the back of the field.

"No – I can't," Jonas said, sadly. Jackie looked at him, then back to the field.

"But they're right there!" But Jonas just shook his head. Jackie understood and just followed him into the house. The time for Jonas to be able to see fairies had passed.

After Jackie had washed and changed, she returned to the kitchen where Jonas had made her a feast. She took her first bite of the most delicious bologna sandwich ever made, and Jonas went to get their parents. When Polt and Effy could hear the happy voices of the Staples family coming from the kitchen, they felt that they could go home themselves.

"Will you go back here?" Polt asked Effy.

She thought for a moment, which was not like Effy. "I've had a lot of happy times in that garden," she said, carefully. "Some day, perhaps, but not for a while, I have to think some things through." Polt smiled knowing that all the thinking in the world wouldn't keep Effy from finding more trouble to get into. He also knew that he'd be there to help her get back out again. They turned away from Jackie's home, and headed back to their own.

As for Jackie and Samantha, all fall they decorated their notebooks with fairies, wrote stories about fairies, and read books about fairies. They even wandered the woods hoping to find the fairy spring. When the weather turned cold, club meetings, swim lessons, cookie baking and sleepovers began. It's not that they had forgotten the fairies, it's just that the world is full of many wonderful things. Their love of fairies had sort of moved aside to let some other things in. Besides, there was always next summer.

The End

About the Author

I live in Auburn, Maine with my husband, son and two cats. I have been following the lives of fairies on the magical Merrill Hill since I first explored the woods behind my house.

I had a life changing adventure when I taught English as a Foreign Language at Chonbuk National University in Korea for two years the 1980's. Being one of a handful of westerners in a city of a half million, when you can't speak or read the language, really shows you what you are made of. Later on, back home in Maine, I became a middle school language arts teacher; I love the wackiness of middle schoolers! In the 1990's I began working with polymer clay and for a short time had a jewelry business. My love of polymer clay evolved into making fairies and writing about fairies naturally followed. You can see my fairy creations on facebook at *Mary's Fairies*.

Thank you for reading my book!

Mary Savignano Gagnon

Made in the USA
Las Vegas, NV
06 May 2021